CUBAN CROCODILE
Crocodylus rhomfifer   Cuba

Winston's friends at the Reptile House

Nancy Winslow Parker

WORKING FROG

GREENWILLOW BOOKS · NEW YORK

FOR BEATRICE GAUNTT PARKER

The author wishes to thank William Holmstrom and Kathy Gerety of the Herpetology
Department of the New York Zoological Society for their help in the preparation of this book

CONTENTS

The Pond

My name is Winston. I am a seven-inch,
one-pound Bullfrog. I work at the zoo.
I would like to tell you about my life.
One summer evening several years ago,
I was sitting by a small pond enjoying
the night air. Only a few stars could be
seen in the sky. It was very still. Not far
away, I could see a tiny light bobbing and
twinkling—too low for a star, too small for
the moon. It came closer and closer.

In no time at all the light was shining directly in my eyes. I blinked, croaked "jug-o-rum," and was about to escape whatever it was by jumping into the pond when, *thump!*, a large net was thrown over me.

"Gotcha," exclaimed a deep voice. I found myself hanging over the pond in a dripping net. Then I was lifted gently out of the net and placed in a wet bag. I croaked in alarm, but it was too late....

The bag was quickly tied at the top, placed in a Styrofoam cooler, and set on the front seat of a truck.

I was driven off into the night.

The Zoo

The next morning I was taken to the Bronx Zoo by Bill, the man who had captured me at the pond. He works at the zoo's Reptile House, which holds all the amphibians and reptiles— that's salamanders, toads, frogs, lizards, snakes, turtles, crocodiles, and alligators.

Bill carried the cooler into a back room at the Reptile House.

He took the lid off the cooler and untied the
wet bag. I hopped out and landed with a *plop*
on a table top. Some people who worked at
the zoo crowded around to see me. They said
"Ooh" and "Aah."

I was immediately given a number, which was written on a card along with my place of origin—Witchett's Pond, Westchester County, New York. The card also noted that I was caught by William Holmstrom of the New York Zoological Society on July 18.

Next I was examined. I didn't know why I was there, but I let the keepers go ahead with their work. They looked over my skin for punctures or tears, and a stool sample was sent to the lab to be checked for parasites.

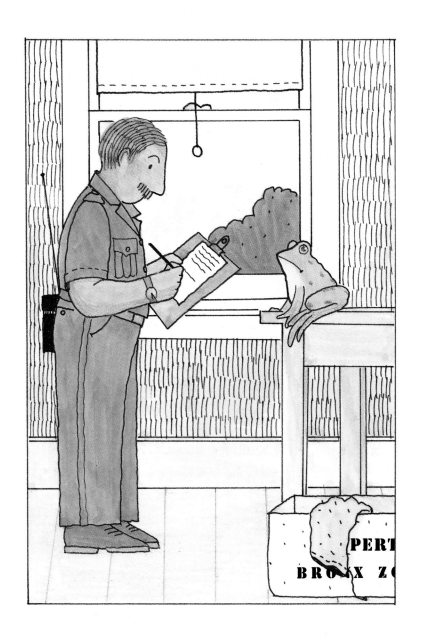

Then I was weighed and my body measured
from tip of nose to vent. I am sorry they didn't
measure my legs, too, as they are especially long
and well developed, but legs are not included in
a frog's measurements.

Each week I was to be fed a diet of twenty crickets, one goldfish, and one mouse. The keepers were wise enough to know that I prefer my foods alive and eat them whole.

TANK: #6   Temp. 71°

NAME: Winston (Bullfrog)

Acq. No.: 3952

DATE	DIET	ATE	NOTES

Finally I was placed in a holding tank in another back room. The tank contained one rock and some plastic leaves. I kept wondering why I was there.

The Holding Tank

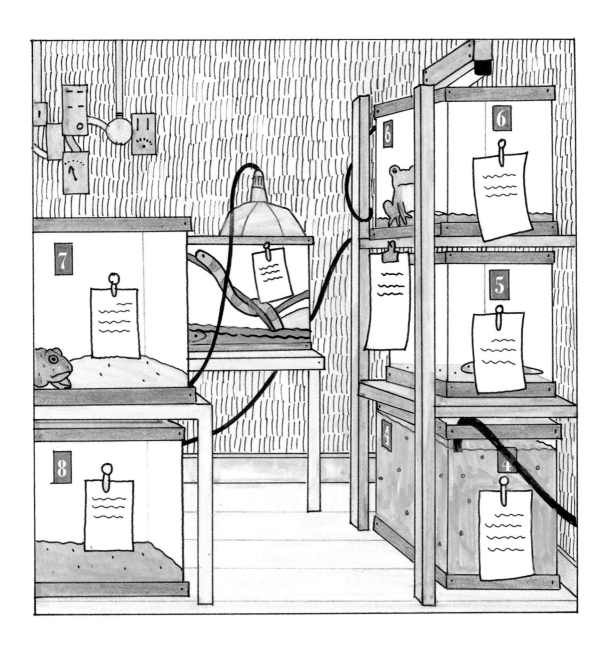

My holding tank was on a shelf among other similar tanks. After I calmed down, I looked around at some of my neighbors....

7/13	5 worms		
7/14	4 goldfish	ate all	
7/15	1ˢ mouse	ate all	opaque shed
7/16	6 goldfish	ate 4	

Just to the right were some Northern Water Snakes from Lake Erie,

5/14	6 worms	6	
5/15	1^s mouse	1	
5/17	3 crickets	ate all	eye closed

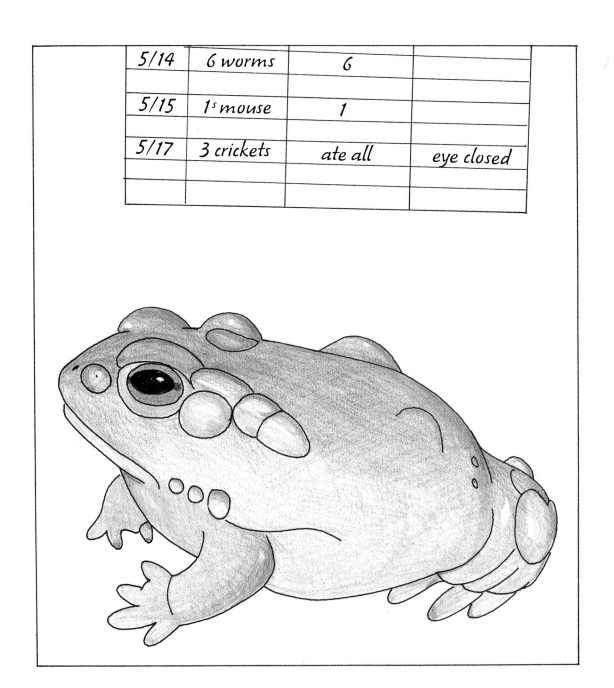

and across the aisle, a sullen Colorado River Toad, who had recently arrived from Arizona.

5/15	3 crickets			
5/17	6 crickets	ate all		

Under the toad's tank were several small Tomato Frogs, native to Madagascar, all hiding under moss. Heavy screens were attached to the tops of all the tanks.

These neighbors were all strangers to my former pond life. Not one of them paid any attention to me.

Although these surroundings were of some interest, this was not home. There were no thick reeds to hide in, no cool mud to squat in, no damp moss to sit on. Lonely and bored, I fell asleep.

At the end of the day Bill came to see me with some visitors. He told the visitors that this was the area where the Reptile House kept some of their "back-ups." These back-ups, he said, are the toads, frogs, snakes, and turtles who one day will replace those who are removed from display at the zoo for various reasons.

I couldn't believe my ears.

On display!

AT THE ZOO!

Bill told the visitors that the Northern Water Snakes were there to replace some Waxy Tree Frogs (frogdom's champion escape artists) who had squeezed under the screening at the top of their tank and hopped out of the zoo forever.

In another tank the new Colorado River Toad's sociability was being tested, as the one currently on exhibit was so shy that he burrowed under the sand in his tank and stayed there all day long. It was a great disappointment to toad-lovers who came from all over the city to see him.

It was then that I heard my name mentioned and my fate decided. I was to replace a Bullfrog who had become so stressed out by the number of visitors peering into his tank that he had refused to eat. He was taken to the place where he had been found—a cranberry bog in the New Jersey Pine Barrens—and let go.

After Bill and the visitors left, I thought about what I was supposed to do and why I was there. I was too upset to eat the crickets Bill had left for me. I spent the next few days sleeping or watching my neighbors: the Northern Water Snakes, the Colorado River Toad, and the plump Tomato Frogs sitting stupidly on the moss in their tank.

Bill came to check me every day. At the end of three weeks I had recovered my former appetite and had eaten a large goldfish and one gray mouse. My coloring was a handsome green, and my throat a golden yellow. Bill said I was ready to be moved into the display tank to begin my life as a working frog.

Early the next morning, before the zoo was open to the public, Bill arrived to prepare my new tank. First he placed a large rock in a corner of the tank, on the edge of a tiny pond. Then he planted my favorite reeds and grasses by the water and poked clumps of damp moss under the leaves. Special lighting was hooked up over the display, and the tank temperature was set at 70 degrees Fahrenheit. Then Bill placed me in my new home.

BULLFROG
Rana catesbeiana

· NOTICE ·
**DO NOT
TAP
ON GLASS**

I had to admit, everything looked just like my former pond. I felt good, too, but a little nervous about my new job. I shouldn't have been, because in a few minutes the Reptile House doors were opened to the public and the daily visitors swarmed in.

I sat quietly on the corner rock, blinking from time to time, and when the desire to show off arose, I drew air into my nose, which made my throat puff out a lot.

"Eek!" shouted a visitor. "Look at those eyes," another yelled. Someone tapped excitedly on the glass. "**NOT ALLOWED,**" ordered a guard.

By the end of my first day of work, 87 boys, 59 girls, and 108 mothers, fathers, and teachers had peered in at me. After closing time Bill came by to see me. He rearranged some of the plants in my tank. When he put me back in the tank, he gave me a few extra crickets.

Since coming to the Reptile House, I have not missed one day of work. Each day is different—new faces, new hats, new coats. When things are slow, I can look across the room at my neighbors, the Giant Toad, the Reticulated Python, and the Timber Rattlesnake.

And Bill comes by every day, sometimes with a fat cricket or a wriggling worm for me, Winston—Working Frog.

Library of Congress Cataloging-in-Publication Data
Parker, Nancy Winslow.
    Working frog / by Nancy Winslow Parker.
        p.   cm.
    Summary: Winston the bullfrog describes his life at the Reptile
House at the Bronx Zoo.
    ISBN 0-688-09918-1. ISBN 0-688-09919-X (lib. bdg.)
    1. Frogs—Juvenile fiction. [1. Frogs—Fiction. 2. Zoos—Fiction.]
I. Title.   PZ10.3.P2275Wo   1992   [E]—dc20
90-24173   CIP   AC

CUBAN CROCODILE
Crocodylus rhomfifer   Cuba

Winston's friends at the Reptile House